MS WIZ SMELLS A RAT

Terence Blacker writes for children and adults. In addition to the best-selling *Ms Wiz* stories, his children's books include *The Transfer*, *Homebird*, the *Hotshots* series, *The Great Denture Adventure* and *Nasty Neighbours/Nice Neighbours*.

What the reviewers have said about *Ms Wiz*:

"Every time I pick up a Ms Wiz, I'm totally spellbound . . . a wonderfully funny and exciting read." *Books for Keeps*

"Hilarious and hysterical." Susan Hill, *Sunday Times*

"Terence Blacker has created a splendid character in the magical Ms Wiz. Enormous fun." *The Scotsman*

"Sparkling zany humour . . . brilliantly funny." *Children's Books of the Year*

ary

D0242712

Titles in the Ms Wiz series

Terence Blacker

Ms Wiz
Smells a Rat

Illustrated by Tony Ross

MACMILLAN
CHILDREN'S BOOKS

For Jack Bardwell

Acknowledgement

I would like to thank Niall Bole of Holy Rosary
Primary School, Belfast, for helping me with the
title for this book.

First published 1998 by Macmillan Children's Books

This edition published 1999 by Macmillan Children's Books
a division of Macmillan Publishers Limited
25 Eccleston Place, London SW1W 9NF
Basingstoke and Oxford
www.macmillan.com

Associated companies throughout the world

ISBN 0 330 37466 4

A CIP catalogue record for this book is available from
the British Library.

Phototypeset by Intype London Ltd
Printed and bound in Great Britain by Mackays of Chatham plc, Kent

CHAPTER ONE

An Early Morning Bite

It was early one summer's morning and Ms Wiz was in bed with her husband, Mr Arnold. They both had a busy day ahead of them – Mr Arnold was inspecting a school and Ms Wiz was trying to write the story of her life, *There's No Business Like Ms Wizness: The Memoirs of a Paranormal Operative*, as well as look after their baby William, who right now was sleeping in the next room.

But, just for a few moments, as the sun streamed through a gap in the curtains and the birds sang in the garden outside, they were relaxed.

"Heigh-ho." Mr Arnold reached for his spectacles on the bedside table. "Another lovely day."

Slowly, he pulled back the duvet and swung his legs out of bed. Sleepily, he felt for his slippers with his feet.

"AAAAGGGHHHH!"

Mr Arnold's scream shattered the peace of the morning. He leapt high in the air, his legs pedalling wildly. When he came down, he was standing on the bed, staring wide-eyed down at the floor.

"That bloomin', blinkin' . . . blastin' creature." With a shaking hand, Mr Arnold pointed downwards. "It bit me."

"Bit you?" Frowning, Ms Wiz peered over the edge of the bed, and smiled. "Oh, Herbert."

From the warm depths of Mr Arnold's slipper, a brown and white rat looked up, blinking. "Well, thank you very much," said Herbert the rat. "What a *lovely* wake-up call that was – a great big smelly foot coming down on me. *So* kind, I must say."

"I thought I asked you not to sleep in Brian's slipper." Ms Wiz tried to sound severe but somehow she was unable to keep the laughter out of her voice.

"I was lonely," said Herbert.

"And you know that you should never ever bite people."

"It wasn't a bite," said Herbert. "I was yawning and your husband decided to put his toe in my mouth." He gave a ratty shudder. "Not pleasant."

Mr Arnold sat down on the bed and turned his back deliberately on Herbert. "Dolores, I just cannot stand it any more." He spoke with the quiet dignity of a man about to make an important announcement. "Do you recall what I asked you on the day we got married?"

"You asked me to love and honour you until death do us—"

"*Apart* from that."

"Ah." Ms Wiz thought hard.

"Maybe . . . something about magic?" she said eventually.

"Precisely. We agreed that there would be no spells – that this house would be a magic-free zone. Now, what would you call a talking rodent who follows me about, eats my chocolate biscuits, complains about the TV programmes I like to watch and tells me I'm putting on weight every time I get in the bath? If that's not magic, what is?" Mr Arnold crossed his arms. "There are three of us in this marriage. It's getting a bit crowded."

"I'll ask him to behave," said Ms Wiz.

"Behave? That yellow-toothed, long-tailed hooligan? Forget it," said Mr Arnold. "I want him out."

"But Brian," said Ms Wiz. "He's been with me through thick and thin."

"And guess who the thick was," muttered Herbert.

Mr Arnold ignored him. "Either

that rat goes or I do," he said.

"Toodle-oo then," said Herbert. "Nice knowing you."

"Oh Herbert," murmured Ms Wiz sadly. "What am I going to do with you?

In the Harris household, Friday evenings were special. At seven o'clock Mr Harris would ring the local Italian takeaway and ask for three large pizzas to be delivered. At half past seven, the whole family – Mr Harris, Mrs Harris and their only son, Peter, who was known to his friends as Podge – would sit down to watch their favourite programme, *The Avenue*.

"This is what family life is all about," said Mr Harris, as they settled down with their pizzas that Friday night. "I've been working hard all week, you two have been messing around, doing whatever

you do. Now we can relax together – it's lovely."

"Yes." Mrs Harris smiled. "We are a lovely family, aren't we?"

"Family?" Mr Harris looked slightly surprised. "I was talking about the pizza. American Hot – my favourite."

It was at that moment that the front doorbell rang.

"Peter," said Mr Harris without taking his eyes off the television.

Podge put his pizza aside and made his way to the front door.

On the doorstep was a stooped figure in ragged clothes, a battered old cap on her head and a bright red scarf which hid most of her face. Over her arm, she carried a large basket.

"Apples, young man?" she croaked. "Very fresh, very cheap."

"No, thanks," said Podge.

"You won't regret it." The woman seemed to wink. "They've got a special ingredient added. It's called Herbert." She held out a paper bag and, for the first time, Podge noticed the black nail-varnish on her fingers.

"Ms Wiz?" he whispered.

Ms Wiz put a finger to her lips. "I need you to look after Herbert," she said

in a low voice. "Just for a bit."

"Herbert? But my dad hates—"

"What does your dad hate?" Behind Podge, Mr Harris appeared in the hall, his mouth greasy from pizza. "And who's Herbert?"

Podge hesitated, thinking fast.

"Sherbet!" he said suddenly. "I was just saying that you couldn't stand sherbet." He grabbed the bag from Ms

Wiz. "No, we certainly don't want any sherbet apples in this house, thank you very much. But we'll take these." Clutching the paper bag, he closed the door quickly. "Sherbet apples," he said to his father. "What will they think of next?"

But Mr Harris was still staring at the door. "I'm sure I've seen that woman somewhere before."

CHAPTER TWO

A Bit Rattled

Moments later, Podge was closing the bedroom door behind him, carefully laying the paper bag on his bed. It crackled and moved for a moment. Then, with some difficulty, Herbert the rat squeezed himself between two apples and emerged into the light, blinking.

"Humans get huge lorries and vans when they move house," he grumbled. "What do I get? A paper bag full of old apples."

"Is that you, Herbert?" asked Podge.

Herbert sighed wearily. "Get a lot of talking rats round here, do you? Lots of intelligent rodents delivered in bags of apples by women wearing black nail-varnish and talking in a silly voice?"

"No need to be sarcastic," said Podge. "What was that you said about moving house?"

The rat sniffed. "Booted out of my very own home with not so much as a toothbrush."

"Toothbrush?" Podge glanced at Herbert's brownish teeth. "I never realized you used a—"

"Never mind, I'll share yours," said Herbert casually.

Podge gulped. "I don't want to sound rude," he said, quickly changing the subject. "But what exactly are you doing here?"

"Search me, old bean." Herbert the rat pointed his nose in the direction of the paper bag. "I believe there's some kind of note from Her Royal Ms Wizness."

Podge reached into the bag. Wedged between two apples was a piece of paper, the corner of which had been badly nibbled. Carefully, he unfolded the note and read it to himself.

Dear Podge

*I've got a bit of a problem at home.
You couldn't be a love and look after
Herbert for while, could you? You were
always his favourite at St Barnabas.
He's no trouble but remember to leave
a window open at night – he likes
to wander about. I'll be in touch when
I've sorted things out. Thanks a
million.*

Your old pal, Ms Wiz

*PS I'm sorry about turning up
disguised as an apple-seller.
I promised Brian I wouldn't use
any magic.*

*PPS Herbert likes the special fancy
rat mixture you can get at pet shops.*

PPPS *And chocolate biscuits for a treat.*

PPPPS *He seems to be a bit grumpy at the moment – can't think why.*

PPPPPS *Give him a big kiss from me and tell him I'm missing him already.*

"What did she say?" asked Herbert, trying to look casual and uninterested.

Podge hesitated. "She says she's missing you and she's asked me to give you a big kiss."

"Ugh, kiss a human?" Herbert leapt back. "You must be joking."

"I don't believe it." Podge stared at Ms Wiz's note, shaking his head.

"Oh, all right, I'll kiss you if it means so much to you," said Herbert.

"Eh? No, I meant this whole idea of you staying here. My parents can't stand animals. When I won a goldfish at a fair, I had to give it away because my mum didn't like the way it looked at her. My dad's idea of a good time is throwing stones at cats who come into the garden."

"Sensible man," said Herbert. "Nasty, unfriendly creatures, they are."

"But a rat in this house?" Podge groaned. "It's a nightmare."

"Not just any rat, old bean," said Herbert. "I am a bit special."

"And that makes it worse," said Podge. "Dad hates magic almost as much as he hates animals."

Herbert sighed. "Well, you'll just have to hide me," he said firmly. "A drawer will do. With nice warm, woollen socks – clean socks, if you don't mind."

From downstairs, Podge heard his mother calling his name. "All right," he sighed. "But I'd better go now. My pizza will be getting cold."

"Mm, pizza, my favourite," said Herbert.

He hopped towards Podge.

It was a particularly good episode of *The Avenue* that night. There were two arguments and a minor car crash, a wedding was cancelled at the last minute and someone got punched on the nose.

But Podge was too tense to enjoy it. Sitting on the edge of the sofa, eating his pizza, all he could think of was what had happened that evening.

Ms Wiz. The note. Herbert.

What would his dad say if he discovered that, not only had a talking rat come to stay, but at that very moment, it was hiding inside Podge's shirt?

"What's the matter, Peter?" his mother asked in a concerned tone of voice. "You're looking a bit peaky."

"Nothing," said Podge. "I just feel a bit . . . rattled this evening."

"Oh, very good joke," murmured Herbert from his hiding place.

"What was that?" said Mrs Harris.

"Must have been my stomach rumbling," said Podge quickly.

"I'm not surprised it's rumbling." Mr Harris glanced across at his son. "You haven't even finished your pizza. Give it here then – I think I've just got room for it."

"Er, no. I'll . . . eat it in a moment."

"I don't know what's the matter with you these days," grumbled Mr Harris. "I remember when all you needed was a takeaway and a bit of telly and you'd be happy all evening. These days, it's books and questions and homework and you don't even eat up your food."

Podge was just thinking of a reply when something made him sit up very straight in his chair. Inside his shirt, Herbert was on the move. Before Podge could do anything, a tiny rat's arm appeared between the buttons of his shirt. It pointed at the remains of the pizza and made a brisk beckoning gesture.

Quickly, Podge covered his stomach with both hands. "I think I'll just warm this up in the oven," he said, standing up carefully. Before his parents could

say anything, he hurried out to the kitchen, carrying his plate. Wrapping the slice of pizza in a paper towel, he went upstairs to his room.

"Are you crazy, Herbert?" he said, taking the rat out from his shirt.

"I only wanted some pizza," said Herbert. "I wouldn't have minded watching a bit of telly either."

"My dad would go mad if he saw you."

Herbert looked away unhappily. "Funny how everyone seems to have gone off one these days. Your parents. That silly Mr Arnold. Even Ms Wiz has abandoned me. I can't understand what it is about a talking rat that people seem so uncomfortable with." He gave a long, thin sigh.

Podge stroked Herbert's head. "I'm comfortable with you," he said. "It's just that we'll have to be a bit careful now that you're staying here." He put the slice of pizza down in front of Herbert. "Eat up. It's American Hot."

"Has it got cheese?" Herbert asked in a sulky voice. "I *must* have cheese on my pizzas."

"Peter!" From downstairs, the booming voice of Mr Harris could be heard.

"Now what?" moaned Podge to himself.

"*Peter*!" Mr Harris raised his voice.

"These apples – something's been nibbling at them."

Podge groaned. "Gee thanks, Herbert," he said. "That's all I need."

Herbert was lying back on the bed, chewing slowly on his pizza, a smile on his face. "You know," he said. "I think I could get to like it here."

CHAPTER THREE

Arabella

Rats are charming, easygoing creatures. Give them space, a nice run and lots of food and they'll be happy. Hamsters, gerbils and guinea pigs are all right in their way but most sensible people would agree that there's no pet quite as perfect in every way as a rat.

On the other hand, a magical talking rat who's in a rather bad mood and who's being hidden from parents who can't stand any kind of animal can sometimes be a bit of problem.

Yet, for about three weeks, Herbert's stay with Podge Harris passed without too much trouble.

When Podge insisted that his mother knocked on the door before entering his room, Mrs Harris thought it was just part of growing up.

When Mr Harris noticed that his favourite chocolate biscuits were disappearing, he assumed that Podge was the culprit.

When Lizzie, Podge's friend from Class Five at St Barnabas, took to coming round after school, Podge explained that they were doing homework together and his parents believed every word.

Neither Mr nor Mrs Harris had the faintest idea that Herbert the rat was now living in the bottom drawer of a cupboard where Podge used to keep his old toys. He had made a nest out of an old tracksuit and had carefully gnawed a hole in the back of the cupboard so that he could get in and out whenever he chose.

Podge had spent his pocket money on the fancy rat mix which Ms Wiz had mentioned and every day would bring Herbert a treat from downstairs – some cornflakes, a bit of cake or, best of all, a chocolate biscuit.

As Ms Wiz had suggested, Podge had left open the window of his bedroom, so that at night Herbert could slip out of the house, across the roof and down into the outside world. Sometimes, early in the morning, Podge would feel him tiptoeing across the bed on his return to his drawer.

Until, one morning, he didn't.

"Maybe he's run back to Ms Wiz," said Lizzie when she returned with Podge after school that day. Lizzie knew everything about animals and, of all his friends in Class Five, she had taken most interest in Herbert.

Podge shook his head. "He would have told me," he said, gazing sadly at

the empty drawer. "Perhaps he's been run over. Or got lost. What am I going to tell Ms Wiz?"

For a moment, they sat in gloomy silence. Then a sound, only slightly louder than thought, could be heard from across the room. It was a sort of humming noise and came from behind the half-closed door of a large wardrobe.

Podge and Lizzie looked at one another, then slowly approached the wardrobe. When Podge opened the door, they saw in the darkness, the pale figure of Herbert, stretched out in one of Podge's old trainers. Around his neck was a chain of forget-me-nots.

"Hi," he said dreamily.

"Where have you been, Herbert?" asked Podge. "We were so worried about you."

"If you were going to stay out the night, at least you could have told us," said Lizzie. "We were out of our minds with worry."

"You treat this place like a hotel," said Podge. "I never thought you'd be so irresponsible."

"It's not so much that you've let us down," said Lizzie. "It's that you've let yourself down. We're very disappointed."

Herbert looked coolly from Podge to Lizzie and back again. "Thank you, Mummy and Daddy," he said.

"And what are you doing in the cupboard?" asked Lizzie.

"We thought it looked cosier in here," said Herbert sleepily. "Now, if you don't mind, I'd like to catch up on my kip."

"*We*?" said Podge and Lizzie together.

It was at this moment that, from another shoe nearby, a second pair of ears emerged nervously, shyly. In the half-light, Podge and Lizzie could see another rat – one that was quite unlike Herbert. It was greyer, darker and with no white on it – the sort of rat you might see scurrying along a ditch or across a road late at night.

"Podge," muttered Lizzie beneath her breath. "I think that's a wild rat."

"Meet my new girlfriend," said Herbert proudly. "I've called her Arabella."

"Arabella?" said Podge politely. "Very posh."

"Just because she doesn't talk like you and me." Herbert's little eyes blazed angrily. "Just because she was born in a sewer, you think you can laugh at her."

"We weren't laughing," said Lizzie. "It's just that fancy rats and feral rats aren't meant to mix. I read it in a book."

"She is a bit of a wild child, it's true," said Herbert. "That's what I like about her. I'll teach her how to talk and she'll bring out my inner warrior." He smiled

at Arabella, who was staring at him with adoring eyes. She gave a little squeak of admiration.

"I think the talking might be a bit of problem," murmured Podge.

"She's different from you." Lizzie spoke gently, not wanting to hurt Herbert's feelings. "She'll probably have . . . fleas and things."

Herbert shrugged.

"What are a few blood-sucking parasites when true love comes to call?

You know what they say – love me, love my fleas." He placed a paw on his heart and gave a little cough. "In fact, I'm writing a little song for Arabella. Would you like to hear it?"

Without waiting for an answer, he began to sing in a thin, quavery voice.

"My love was born down in a sewer,
She's come up from the gutter.
She's ripe and tasty and mature,
Like cheese on bread and butter.

"Every day I love to—"

Just then there was a sharp knock on the door. Herbert and Arabella dived back into their trainers. As Mrs Harris entered, Podge shut the wardrobe door.

"You two are meant to be doing homework." Podge's mother looked around the room suspiciously. "I thought I heard some singing."

"Music," said Podge quickly. "We've been asked to write a song together."

"Go on then," said Mrs Harris. "Let's hear you."

Podge took a deep breath. "La-la-la, tum-ty-tum, blah, blah," he sang tunelessly.

"We're sort of still working on it," said Lizzie.

"Anyway, I need to clean your room," said Mrs Harris. "Something rather unpleasant seems to have happened."

Podge winced. "Unpleasant?"

"It's a bit embarrassing to have to say this in front of a nice girl like Lizzie but . . . there seems to be an invasion of mice in the house. Or maybe" – Mrs Harris shuddered – "even rats."

"Rats, yuk!" said Podge loudly, glancing in the direction of the cupboard. "How d'you know?"

"There are droppings all over the kitchen table – near the biscuits. Your dad's called in the Environmental Health Officer to deal with them. Rats in our own little house." Shaking her head, Mrs Harris turned to leave. "Who would have believed it?"

For a few seconds after the door had closed, Podge and Lizzie stood in silence.

"Did you hear that, Herbert?" Podge said quietly.

From behind the cupboard door, a faint sound of singing could be heard.

"Every day I love to think
Of my own sweet Arabella."

"Herbert?" said Lizzie.

"Her little eyes of—"

"Herbert!" said both Podge and Lizzie.

There was a moment's silence. "Ah

yes," Herbert mumbled in a voice that was almost embarrassed. "That was the other thing about Arabella I forgot to mention. Um . . . She's not exactly house-trained."

CHAPTER FOUR

Love Potion Number Nine

"I'm missing her *so* much. I'm missing her from the tip of my front whiskers to the end of my tail. I'm only half a rat without her. I'm a mere shadow of my rodent self."

"Give it a break, Herbert," muttered Podge.

From his position in Podge's top pocket, Herbert the rat was talking about love as they made their way down the High Street with Lizzie.

"Just concentrate on getting us to Ms Wiz's house," said Lizzie. "Forget about Arabella for a moment."

"I wouldn't be missing her so much if you'd brought her with us," said Herbert grumpily.

"Sorry, Herb," said Podge. "Call me

old-fashioned but I'm not walking around with a street rat in my pocket."

"She's no more a street rat than you're a street child," said Herbert.

"Except I don't live in a sewer and poo on the kitchen table," muttered Podge under his breath.

"Next left!" snapped Herbert.

They walked down a quiet, leafy side street and soon were standing outside a small house, covered in ivy, which Podge recognized from the last time he had visited Ms Wiz. He rang the bell and, seconds later, the door was flung open.

"Podge! Lizzie!" Ms Wiz glanced down and her smile wavered slightly. "Herbert! What a lovely surprise. How have you been?"

Herbert cleared his throat, took a deep breath and began to sing.

"My love's a rat beyond compare.
Beside her, others pale.

I want to kiss her everywhere,
From her whiskers to her tail."

"Herbert's fallen in love," Podge
explained. "And his girlfriend's living
with him in my house."

"Oh, Herbert, really." Ms Wiz
laughed.

"She's cute and clean and healthy too,
Entirely free from rabies.
What's more, in a week or two,
She's going to have our babies."

"*What!*" said Podge.

"Blimey, that was quick," said Lizzie.

"You wouldn't understand." Herbert shrugged. "It's a rat thing."

"My parents have discovered there are rats in the house," Podge told Ms Wiz. "They've called in the Environmental Health Officer."

"The world is against us but we don't care." Herbert was waving his paws around. "Love will conquer all."

Ms Wiz shook her head. "I'm not sure there's much I can do." Glancing over her shoulder, she dropped her voice. "I promised Brian I wouldn't get involved in any magic."

"Excuse me, Ms Wiz," said Podge

firmly. "You can't just deliver Herbert to me, get me into all sorts of trouble and then just wash your hands of it."

"*So* selfish," said Herbert. "Always was, always will be."

Ms Wiz thought for moment. "Wait," she said, turning back into the house. When she returned, she held a small bottle in her hand. "Put a drop of this liquid in the rat man's tea," she said. "I call it 'Love Potion Number Nine'."

"Is that because it's got nine magic ingredients?" asked Podge.

"Or is nine a special paranormal number?" asked Lizzie.

"No, it's just named after a song I used to sing when I was ... slightly younger," said Ms Wiz.

"What does it—?"

"Sshh." Ms Wiz put a finger to her lips. "I'm sure everything will be just fine," she said, and closed the front door in their face.

"What did I tell you?" said Herbert. "It's just 'me, me, me' with that woman."

It wasn't a great plan. It wasn't even a particularly original one. But, in the end, it was the only plan that Podge and Lizzie could think of.

They would hide Herbert and Arabella in the wardrobe. They would try to get the Environmental Health Officer to take some tea. They would slip a drop of the potion Ms Wiz had given them into his cup. Then they would hope for the best.

"I'm sure it will work," said Podge as he closed the wardrobe door on the two rats.

"We just have to trust Ms Wiz," said Lizzie.

"Hah!" The voice of Herbert could be heard through the door. "That's the mistake I made. Now look where I am."

At that moment, they heard the front doorbell ring. "Don't say a word," said Podge in the general direction of the wardrobe.

By the time they had gone downstairs, a small, chubby man with a moustache had been shown into the kitchen. "Ken Duff's the name," he was saying to Mr and Mrs Harris. "I'm the council's Environmental Health Officer."

"Excellent," said Podge's father. "There are rats in the house and I want them dead." He held up a saucer on which some small droppings had been kept.

Mr Duff lowered his nose and sniffed at them. "Could be bats," he said uncertainly.

"Bats in the kitchen, eating my chocolate biscuits? Don't talk daft," said Mr Harris.

"Kettle's boiling," said Podge as

casually as he could manage. "Anyone fancy a cup of tea?"

"I'm sure Mr Duff's too busy for tea," said Mr Harris. "He's got some rats to deal with."

"Thirsty work," said Lizzie.

"Actually . . ." The Environmental Health Officer smiled at Podge and Lizzie. "A cup of tea would go down very nicely."

"Yesss!" said Podge. "I mean . . . yes, would you like sugar with it?"

"Just one spoonful," said Mr Duff.

"What d'you use?" asked Mr Harris. "Gas? Guns? Dynamite? I'll help if you want."

Mr Duff looked shocked. "Oh no, I'll just leave a little powder in the places where they feed. When they eat it, they'll go slowly to sleep."

"Tea?" Podge handed him the cup.

Mr Duff sipped at the tea and smiled.

"Mm," he said. "Does you good, doesn't it?"

"Hope so," murmured Podge.

At first, it was difficult to see how exactly Love Potion Number Nine worked. There was no strange humming noise. Mr Duff didn't change in any dramatic way after drinking the tea. He just smiled a bit more.

"No rats here." He sounded almost relieved as he emerged from the sitting room.

"What about upstairs?" asked Mrs Harris. "Peter's room is such a mess it would be heaven for a rat."

"Actually, they're rather tidy animals," said Mr Duff, heading up the stairs.

By the time he had reached Podge's room, he had begun to act rather

strangely. He looked at the clothes on the floor, at the pile of papers on the desk, at the unmade bed, and smiled broadly. "What a *lovely* room," he said.

"Eh?" said Podge.

As if by instinct, he went straight to the wardrobe and looked down at the shoes. There, trying to make themselves look small, were Herbert and Arabella.

Podge was just about to explain that they were his secret pets when Mr Duff looked more closely at the rats.

"*Sweet*," he murmured. "And I do believe this little darling's pregnant."

"Little darling?" Lizzie glanced at Podge. "I thought you were meant to be ... getting rid of them."

"Get rid of them? What a terrible thought. It's a privilege for you to have those adorable little creatures in the house."

Lizzie glanced at Podge. "I think the

potion might be working," she murmured.

"Any luck?" Mrs Harris put her head around the door as Mr Duff stood up and closed the wardrobe door behind him.

For a moment, he stared at Mrs Harris. Then a bashful smile appeared on his face. "Has anyone told you that you're the most beautiful woman in the world?"

A few moments later, he was thrown out on to the street.

CHAPTER FIVE

Stiff City, Ratwise

It was 3.22 the following afternoon when a white van with darkened windows, marked *Killing Fields Pest Control*, turned into Rylett Road and stopped outside the Harrises' house. Three men in white overalls, baseball caps and heavy boots stepped out and trudged up the garden path.

"Thank goodness you're here," said Mr Harris, who was standing at the front door. "We called out an exterminator from the council but they sent round a nutter. He fell in love with my wife."

"I thought he was rather nice," said Mrs Harris from the hall. "He had gentle eyes."

"Never mind gentle eyes," said the

smallest of the three men. "My name's Dave Fields. In the trade, they call me 'Killing' Fields."

Podge appeared at the front door, a mug in his hands. "The kettle's just boiled, Mr . . . er, Killing," he said. "D'you fancy a cup of tea?"

"Tea?" Dave Fields laughed nastily. "We're exterminators. We don't drink tea."

"*He* did, my Ken." Mrs Harris was staring into the distance. "He sipped in a very . . . sensitive way."

Ignoring her, Dave Fields scanned the front garden with narrowed eyes. "We're going in hard and we're going in fast," he said. "Gas, poison. Outside the house and in. In ten minutes' time, this place will be Stiff City, ratwise. He pointed to a manhole nearby. "We'll start there."

Beside Podge, Lizzie gave a little moan. Herbert and Arabella had disappeared, there was no sign of Ms Wiz and there seemed little hope of the men falling for the old love potion trick. "Are you sure you wouldn't like some tea?" she said. "It's really—"

She paused. At that moment, a strange humming noise could be heard. It was getting louder all the time.

Together the three men looked down the street.

A shape, a sort of black and yellow cloud, was approaching. Outside the house, it paused and made its way up the garden path, the hum becoming an angry buzz.

"Blimey, wasps," said one of the men. "Where did they come from?"

Podge nudged Lizzie. "Nice one, Ms Wiz," he whispered.

The wasps grew closer, moving to one side of the path. They surrounded the three men, forcing them back towards the van.

"Where are you off to?" shouted Mr Harris. "I thought you were meant to be a hit squad."

Casually, Dave Fields reached through the window of the van. When he faced the wasps, he was carrying a large gas canister.

"Wasp gas." He smiled unpleasantly, pointed it at the swarm of wasps and pressed a button. A grey cloud enveloped the wasps. When it cleared, the buzzing had died down. Where the wasps had been stood a familiar figure, coughing and wiping tears from her eyes.

"Great magic, Ms Wiz," muttered Podge.

"Unfair," wheezed Ms Wiz. "That was gas – it could have been really nasty."

"It's that fruit-seller again," said Mr Harris. "Where did she come from?"

"Clear off, lady." Dave Fields put the gas canister back in the van. "This is men's work."

"Men's work, eh?" From behind Ms Wiz, a humming sound could just be heard. It grew louder and louder . . . then suddenly began to falter, like an engine misfiring, before fading into silence.

Ms Wiz shook her head helplessly. "I seem to be a bit out of practice these days," she muttered. "I had a spell prepared but it doesn't seem to be working."

"Right," said Dave. "We're going in."

"Halt!"

A thin, well-educated voice, coming from just beyond the manhole, cut the air. The three men hesitated.

"Halt!"

And there, on the garden wall, with Arabella beside him, was Herbert. He was standing on his hind legs, one paw on his heart, the other before him, like a rat general addressing his troops before a great battle.

"Am I dreaming, Dave?" said one of the men. "Or is that a talking rat on the wall?"

"Why do you wish to destroy my people – my wife's family?" Herbert raised his voice. "Have they harmed you in any way? No! Rats and men have lived together for thousands of years. You need us. We help clear up the mess humans leave behind."

"Horrid, dirty things," said Mr Harris.

"Dirty?" Herbert put his tiny arm around Arabella. "Does this divine little thing look dirty to you? Will the babies that she is carrying, who one day will call me 'Daddy' – will they be horrid?"

"I've heard enough of this." Dave Fields stepped forward and extended a big gloved hand towards the wall.

Suddenly, with a loud, angry chattering sound, Arabella moved to stand in front of Herbert. Rearing up on her hind legs, eyes blazing, fangs bared, she was a truly terrifying sight.

"So much for the divine little thing," said Lizzie.

Dave Field had turned pale. "Give us a hand, lads," he called over his shoulder.

As the other two men moved forward, Herbert seemed to take a deep breath. He extended both paws – and began to sing.

"Rats in love, rats in love,
We're different yet the same.
Ours is the secret, special love
That dare not squeak its name."

"Aah," said Mrs Harris. "Isn't that sweet?"

"Sweet? It's rubbish," said Mr Harris. But there was a crack in his voice which Podge had never heard before.

"Every day I love to think
Of my lovely Arabella.
Her eyes are of the brightest pink,
Her teeth are shining yellow."

One of the men sniffed. Another
seemed to be wiping something from the
corner of his eye.

"I'll marry her when the sun shines,
I'll marry her in the rain,
And then, when no one's looking,
I'll marry her again."

"I'm off home," said one of the men.
"Me too," said the other.
Dave shrugged. "They're almost

human," he said, turning to Mr Harris. "Sorry, mate. Can't do it."

"Cuthbert." Mrs Harris laid a hand on her husband's arm. "They remind me of us when we were courting."

"What's going on?" Mr Harris shouted angrily as the men returned to their van. "I thought you were meant to be a hit squad."

But, with a slamming of doors and a roar of the engine, the Killing Fields van drew away and was gone.

"Well done, Ms Wiz," smiled Podge.

"Wiz?" Mr Harris narrowed his eyes. "I knew I recognized you from somewhere. You're that Wiz woman who's always causing spells and magic and . . . trouble."

Absent-mindedly, he reached for the mug in Podge's hand.

"Dad . . ." Podge shouted.

But it was too late. Mr Harris drained the lot in three angry gulps.

"Actually, it wasn't me or my magic." Ms Wiz smiled politely. "It was Herbert and Arabella and" – she shrugged helplessly – "true love."

"I told you love conquers all," said Herbert. "Sometimes being right all the time can be positively boring."

"There's one thing it hasn't conquered," said Podge. "And that's the problem of where Herbert and Arabella and all their little babies are going to live."

Ms Wiz gathered up the two rats in her hands. "If they live outside our house and visit us now and then, I'm sure I can convince Brian to change his mind. He's an old romantic at heart."

Herbert held open the fold of Ms Wiz's coat for his wife. "After you, my dear," he said. She scuttled out of sight. Herbert gave a little wave in the direction of Podge and Lizzie. "Toodle-oo, chaps," he said. "Thanks for having us." Then he disappeared.

"See you both soon." Ms Wiz smiled, turning to leave.

"Not so fast, young lady." Mr Harris laid a hand on her shoulder. "I've got something to say to you."

"Dad, she hasn't done you any harm," said Podge.

"Oh, but she has." Mr Harris seemed to be blushing as he gazed at Ms Wiz. "You see . . . I think I've fallen in love with her."

"Oh." Ms Wiz backed away nervously. "That's nice."

"I know it's a bit sudden but it's the real thing." Mr Harris gave a sort of giggle. "I'm in love."

"Isn't that great, Cuthbert?" said Mrs Harris. "I'm in love, too. All I can think about is that sweet Ken Duff."

"I think I'd better be going," said Ms Wiz.

"Hang on," said Podge. "Thanks to

your precious Love Potion Number Nine, we don't have any rats here but we've got a love riot on our hands."

"It'll fade after about a week," said Ms Wiz.

"A *week*?" said Lizzie.

As Ms Wiz closed the garden gate behind her, the voice of Herbert, muffled but happy, could be heard.

"My love was born down in a sewer,
She's come up from the gutter.
She's ripe and tasty and mature
Like cheese on bread and butter."

"Don't go, darling Ms Wiz," Mr Harris called out.

"Ken," murmured Mrs Harris. "I must see my Ken."

"Help," said Podge.

Collect all the titles in the MS WIZ series!

The prices shown below are correct at the time of going to press. However, Macmillan Publishers reserve the right to show new retail prices on covers which may differ from those previously advertised.

TERENCE BLACKER

1.	Ms Wiz Spells Trouble	0 330 34763 2	£2.99
2.	In Stitches with Ms Wiz	0 330 34764 0	£2.99
3.	You're Nicked, Ms Wiz	0 330 34765 9	£2.99
4.	In Control, Ms Wiz?	0 330 34766 7	£2.99
5.	Ms Wiz Goes Live	0 330 34869 8	£2.99
6.	Ms Wiz Banned!	0 330 34870 1	£2.99
7.	Time Flies for Ms Wiz	0 330 34871 X	£2.99
8.	Power-Crazy Ms Wiz	0 330 34872 8	£2.99
9.	Ms Wiz Loves Dracula	0 330 34873 6	£2.99
10.	You're Kidding, Ms Wiz	0 330 34529 X	£2.99
11.	Ms Wiz, Supermodel	0 330 35312 8	£2.99
12.	Ms Wiz Smells a Rat	0 330 37466 4	£2.99
13.	Ms Wiz and the Sister of Doom	0 330 39173 9	£2.99
14.	Ms Wiz Goes to Hollywood	0 333 90175 4	£9.99

All Macmillan titles can be ordered at your local bookshop or are available by post from:

**Book Service by Post
PO Box 29, Douglas, Isle of Man IM99 1BQ**

Credit cards accepted. For details:
Telephone: 01624 675137
Fax: 01624 670923
E-mail: bookshop@enterprise.net

Free postage and packing in the UK.
Overseas customers: add £1 per book (paperback)
and £3 per book (hardback)